Sheep Amongst Wolves

The Black Circle
Chronicles – Book 4

GARY LEE VINCENT

Burning Bulb
PUBLISHING

Sheep Amongst Wolves
By **Gary Lee Vincent**

Burning Bulb Publishing
P.O. Box 4721
Bridgeport, WV 26330-4721
United States of America
www.BurningBulbPublishing.com

Cover concept by Gary Lee Vincent with photos from Adrien Olichon from Pexels and Jub-Job from Shutterstock.

First Edition.

Paperback Edition ISBN: 978-1-948278-39-3

Printed in the United States of America

DEDICATION

To my band of misfits at Burning Bulb Publishing,
who are blind to the impossible, impervious to the
opinions of the naysayers, and continuously strive to
bring exciting stories to life.
I love you all.

CHAPTER 1

Sunday morning at the Wickenburg, Arizona branch of the Joy of Life Bible Church began just like any other.

People drove into the church premises or walked if they lived close by. It was late summer and the weather was nice. As they entered the church auditorium the parishioners greeted one another and inquired how the week had been. Mothers shepherded their kids to the building at the rear of the auditorium/sanctuary where the children would receive their own Bible lessons.

Assistant pastors Josh and Connie Davis sat on high-backed ministers' chairs at the front of the church, watching the congregation arrive, with ushers directing people left and right into pews.

The young pastoral couple—the husband slim and dark-haired, the wife compact and blonde—were seated to the left of the raised central altar platform. Their seats faced the pulpit, beyond which lay firstly a space for the church's drummer and keyboard player, and then, directly behind that area, there was a similar arrangement of high-backed chairs like those in which Josh and Connie sat for the choir.

Neither the musicians nor the choir were currently out in the auditorium; nor were the Pastor or his wife.

There was a hum of anticipation as the front pews filled up, and soft worship music played from suspended loudspeakers, piped into the building by the church's sound engineers.

All in all, a perfectly normal church morning.

But as he stared at the smiling and expectant faces of the congregation, Josh Davies did not feel happy. He felt the same dissatisfaction that he always did whenever he considered how few this church's congregation were in number.

"You looked bothered, darling," his wife said, laying her hand on his arm. "Is something the matter?"

Connie was sitting on his right; he turned from staring at the largely empty pews to look at her instead. "I can't help it, honey. This church should have a much larger congregation than it does. Yes, they're all on fire for the Lord and that's commendable, but . . . how is that we hardly ever have sixty people for our Sunday morning service?"

Connie nodded understandingly. They'd discussed this many times in the three months since they'd been transferred to this small town. And what made the paltry size of this church's congregation so strange was the fact that the Joy of Life Bible Church was the only church still open in Wickenburg, Arizona. All the other churches—seventeen in total—had shut down in either mysterious or scandalous circumstances over the last four years.

Were something not the matter, one would expect that the displaced congregations of the closed churches would have joined this one, simply to have a place to fellowship afterwards. But according to Pastor Fisher, this hadn't happened once; not one person from any of the shut churches had ever come to join the Joy of Life Bible Church; which, even taking into account differences in denominational doctrine, was really odd.

"This town is really under a heavy demonic oppression," Josh told Connie, "and the sooner we locate the source of it, the better."

Connie gestured across the auditorium to the right-side aisle, where, with a broad smile on her face, red-haired Becky Lowe was steering her motorized wheelchair to the front of the congregation. "I had thought that after the Black Circle had been defeated there would be a lessening of the attacks against this parish, but that's clearly not the case."

No one had seen either Karen or Bill Houston, the Black Circle's agents in Wickenburg, since the night of Becky's exorcism. Becky had said that when she called Karen the next day, Karen had coldly informed her that Bill had fallen ill overnight and she'd had to take him out of town for treatment; and that she had no idea when they would be back in town. Later that day Becky had ridden her wheelchair over to Karen's house to see for herself, and the house had been empty.

There had also been very few recent sightings of the annoying black birds that had plagued the town back then. And those few of the species that had been seen in Wickenburg had avoided the church.

But Josh didn't really think the Black Circle would give up that easily. He knew from experience that they were a tenacious lot, and he had recently begun to suspect that the Black Circle were in Wickenburg for a reason and wouldn't give up the fight until they achieved their aim here.

Frank Everett, the church administrator and also the leader of the church intercessory group, emerged from the vestry ahead of the pastor and his wife. Brother Frank was a large man with short dark hair; the pastor and his wife were both tall and middle-aged and were a friendly-faced couple.

Frank climbed the altar with a solemn tread, tapped the provided microphone to ensure it was working and then said, "Good morning, brothers and sisters, and welcome once more to the house of God. Okay, everyone, let's rise to our feet for a word of prayer."

There was a shuffling of feet, books and handbags as everyone got up. The service had begun.

***

The morning's service proceeded normally for about an hour, with nothing out of the ordinary happening until shortly after Pastor Fisher climbed the altar to begin his sermon.

That was when the black van drove into the church compound.

Momentarily glancing down the left-side aisle, Josh noticed the van as it arrived, but he thought nothing more of it.

"And so, folks," Pastor Fisher was saying, "we really need to understand that the sacrifice that our Lord Jesus made on the cross of Calvary was a

4

complete one, sufficient in every way. No, brothers and sisters, our Lord God never does a shoddy job . . ."

Josh suddenly realized that there was going to be trouble.

Rather than driving into the church parking lot, the black van was instead pulling up alongside the church sanctuary and parking directly in front of the entrance doors, fully blocking the access and egress for the church patrons.

"What on earth is wrong with those ushers?" Connie whispered to Josh. "They know we don't allow vehicles to park there; especially while church is in session."

But the next moment, vehicle noise interrupting the sermon was the least concern of anyone worshipping in the Joy of Life Bible Church on this Sunday morning.

With a loud metal screech, the van's doors slid open and four men leapt out of it, all of them wearing combat fatigues and gloves and with their faces covered by black ski masks. But the most scary detail about the four intruders was that they were all carrying light machine guns.

Oh no! Josh thought, experiencing déjà vu. Two years ago, before he'd become a Christian, the Black Circle had tried to enlist him to shoot up the Tucson branch of the Joy of Life church. Back then only divine intervention had prevented him from carrying out that terrible plan.

And now . . .

"Oh, God, please protect us all," he prayed.

"Jesus!" Connie gasped and leaned against him.

The four men rushed into the church and waved their guns at everyone. There were loud scared whispers from the congregation and choir, and one or two howls of fright, but the armed men didn't start firing. Josh was relieved to see that the intruders were exercising restraint, though how long that would last was anyone's guess.

You didn't bring weapons to a church except you were prepared to use them.

"What do you think you're doing?" Pastor Fisher sputtered angrily from the altar as one of the armed men climbed its steps towards him. "This is the house of God. You can't just—!"

"Shut up." The man shoved the pastor away from the microphone and took his place in front of it.

"Now listen up, everyone," he said in gruff voice. "If even one of you God-bothering idiots thinks of making a phone call, we're going to shoot all of you. *All of you*. Get it?"

Almost everyone in the church nodded. Everyone sat still, not making a move, just staring at the armed men, two of whom walked up and down the aisles, while the third man kept watch on everyone from the front.

"Do what he says, brothers and sisters," Pastor Fisher called down at the congregation. "God will protect us all."

"Shut up, you fool," the masked man on the altar told the pastor, then he turned back to the congregation. "But still, you heard the guy. Don't even think of texting for the police. If you do . . . if we even *hear* the sound of a siren . . ." He finished the sentence by drawing his left thumb across his throat.

Josh sighed in relief. "So, we aren't about to be shot," he whispered to Connie. "Not yet, anyway."

She nodded, her eyes showing her fright. "But what about the two ushers outside on parking attendant duty? This guy has no way of stopping *them* from alerting the police."

Her question was quickly answered when another masked person—this one a woman—pushed both brother Gary and sister Mary into the church before her. She shoved them into one of the middle pews and then walked forward to speak to the man on the altar.

"That accounts for everyone," she told him. "Except for those in the children's church."

"Listen, what do you want?" Pastor Fisher asked the masked man.

"You, Pastor Fisher," the masked man replied. "You're coming with us."

On that revelation, a loud murmur ran through the church.

"No!" Pastor Fisher said, as two of the armed men climbed the altar platform and grabbed him and dragged him down off of it and towards the door through which they'd entered the church. "You can't do this! I'm a servant of God!"

"No, leave my husband!" Madge Fisher protested. "You can't take him away!"

"Shut up, you silly woman," the leader told her and then turned back to the congregation. "Now listen here, you lot." He pointed down at the pastor, who still had disbelief written all over his face. "We've got what we came here for and we're leaving. But be warned: you don't make a phone call to the police for the next thirty minutes. If we hear a single police siren in pursuit before we're two towns away from here, we'll slit Pastor Fisher's throat."

Everyone gasped. Pastor Fisher seemed to sag where he stood, as if he'd been punctured and the fight drained out of him.

The masked man turned and pointed to Connie. "Hey, you there, go over to the children's section and fill in the teachers on what's going on in here. Explain to them in clear and gory detail that if anyone calls for help before we're well away from here, you'll be picking up bits of your pastor's brains from off the sidewalk."

Connie nodded nervously and ran off to do as she'd been instructed. Josh sighed as he watched her go. He looked over at Frank Everett; the church administrator was praying hard under his breath: "Oh, Lord Jesus, deliver Your people now. Keep us all safe from these madmen who dare to profane Your holy temple . . ."

Josh began praying too.

The masked man waved down at the scared church members. "Well, I guess I'll be saying goodbye now, folks. Just remember my warning to you all. Do nothing stupid and no one'll get hurt . . ." He laughed mockingly. "Well not yet, anyway."

And then he climbed down from the pulpit and headed for the church door, while two of the masked gunmen covered his retreat in case someone decided to be a hero.

No one did. Everyone watched helplessly as Pastor Fisher was bundled into the black van and the kidnappers got in after him. And then the van reversed and zoomed off, after making a brief stop to pick up one of their number who had been charged with (they discovered later) stealing the DVR for the church's CCTV cameras.

The whole raid had taken less than ten minutes. The kidnappers had arrived, accomplished their objective and were gone in a flash.

As the van zoomed off, the imposed silence continued in the church, with everyone seeming uncertain what to do, until Josh climbed the altar and addressed the congregation:

"Okay, brothers and sisters, please try to remain calm. Yes, I know you all want to call the cops, but please, please, please, consider our pastor's life. We've no choice but to do what the kidnappers said and wait out their thirty-minute stipulation, or else . .

."

Frank Everett joined Josh at the altar. "But while we're waiting that time out," he said, "let's have a time of prayer and hold up Pastor Fisher before God."

The congregation began praying fervently for the pastor's safety.

Josh took that opportunity to hurry outside and check on Connie in the children's church section.

CHAPTER 2

Police Detective Tom Jenkins of the Wickenburg PD was a large man with thinning dark hair and cold blue eyes. Looking at him one got the impression of a no-nonsense, zero-tolerance character. Detective Jenkins and a team of police investigators arrived at the Joy of Life church ten minutes after the distress call came in. After establishing the core facts of the case, the policemen went to work looking for clues to the kidnappers' identity in and around the church.

Detective Jenkins however, remained with the church leadership: assistant pastors Josh and Connie Davies, church administrator Frank Everett, and Madge Fisher, the abducted man's wife.

At first, they'd been conversing inside the sanctuary, but after a while—sweeping an arm around to indicate the hubbub and milling people—Frank Everett had suggested that they move to one of the rear offices where it was certain to be quieter.

"Everything is so chaotic in here, I can hardly hear myself think," he'd pointed out.

So now they were in one of the rear counselling rooms. The church staff were seated on chairs and desks, while Detective Jenkins stood facing them.

Madge Fisher was clearly just a few steps away from having a nervous breakdown. Her eyes were bloodshot, and her makeup smeared from crying.

"I don't know what they want with my husband!" she repeated over and over again. "Why did they abduct Amos!?" She looked utterly miserable.

Detective Jenkins shook his head. "That's what I'm here to establish, ma'am. And with any luck, we'll quickly apprehend the culprits and restore Pastor Fisher to you and the congregation." He focused his gaze on the distraught woman. "But for the moment, ma'am, I need you to calm down—if you can. I need both you . . ." he looked around at the other church staff, "and everyone else here, to think very hard. Was there anything distinctive that you maybe noticed about the kidnappers? Anything that might give us a clue as to who they might be?"

Everyone was quiet for about a minute after that and then Frank Everett lifted his hand, "If I may, detective?"

Tom Jenkins nodded. "Yeah, please go on."

"Well," Frank said, "I was surprised by how well the kidnappers seemed to know the church."

Josh and Connie looked at him, as did Madge. "Wha-wha-what do you mean?" the pastor's wife asked before the detective could.

Frank looked thoughtful. "It didn't really strike me until the tech guys informed me that they'd also removed the hard disk recorder for the CCTV cameras."

The detective frowned. "What's so odd about that? I'd have thought that would be standard procedure if they wanted to cover their tracks."

Frank nodded, then explained: "Yeah, yeah, sir, but in this case the problem is that we only installed the CCTV unit a month ago."

The detective shrugged. "I still don't get what makes that so strange. To pull off a job like this one in broad daylight and do it successfully, these guys must've been casing your church for a long time. Finding out about the CCTV purchase and installation wouldn't be difficult if they hacked your server."

But Frank Everett shook his head. "No, that's not what I mean. I'll try to clarify. You see, detective, you'll notice that the church doesn't have a security post. So, when we wanted to install the CCTV monitors we had the option of either putting them in one of our own offices, or in the sound engineering booth. We chose the latter option." He shrugged. "We're ministers of the Gospel and none of us wanted to keep staring at the TV screens all day long."

The lawman nodded and Frank went on: "So, the CCTV monitors were installed in the sound engineering booth. The cameras are really just to keep an eye on things during services, so the arrangement works okay, except for one detail: Now as its name suggests, the sound engineering booth is where the sound mixing for the church services is done. The room is packed full of audio equipment—there's a huge mixer that takes up most of the front space, large monitor speakers and audio recorders and also lots of audio processing equipment. So, when we put in the CCTV equipment we had to make compromises as to what would go where." He paused and looked around to ensure that he had everyone's attention.

Detective Jenkins nodded silently, as though the gears of his mind were spinning rapidly.

"Yes, yes, go on, brother Frank!" Madge Fisher said in a desperate voice. "What is all this suspense leading up to!?"

"I'm sorry if I sound long-winded," Frank said, getting to his feet and pacing the room as he explained. "But I had to give a proper background to this, so the detective understands the point I'm trying to make. But yeah, I'll try to finish this quickly. What I'm getting at is this . . . so because there wasn't enough room in the sound engineering booth, we had to split the components up. The two monitors for the CCTV cameras went up against one wall. You can just about make them out from inside the sanctuary." He paused for a few moments, looking from face to face. "No problem there. But the recorder—the DVR—for the cameras presented a problem. There was no space for at in the front of the room because the equipment racks there were already filled up . . . anyway in the end, brother Mike our sound engineer pointed out that we could install the DVR down at the back of the room—there's a cabinet behind the door there for DVDs. Anyway the recorder is right down at the bottom of that cabinet." He stopped pacing and leaned over a desk, staring at everyone. "What I'm getting at is—that that recorder is so concealed that no one could possibly know where it is. And yet, brother Mike said that the man who entered the sound engineering booth didn't even ask them where the DVR was. He just walked in, pointed his gun at them, shut the door behind him and then reached down into the DVD cabinet and yanked the DVR out of there. My question is: how could he—and the kidnappers—have known about the recorder's hidden location . . . ?"

". . . Except someone in the church had informed them of it?" Detective Jenkins filled in for him. "Meaning that this might be an inside job."

Frank Everett nodded at the detective. "Yes, sir, that's exactly what I mean."

Josh and Connie Davies both looked horrified at the information.

"Oh, Jesus, no!" Madge Fisher gasped.

"But surely not?" Connie said.

"I'm afraid so," her husband told her. "Our lord Jesus had twelve apostles and one of them was Judas Iscariot."

Madge Fisher began weeping. "But Judas, in our own church, who . . . who . . . ?"

Connie left her own seat to go comfort the pastor's wife.

"Very, very well put, preacher." Detective Jenkins smiled coldly. "Okay, now, everyone, considering what Mr. Everett has just told us all, I've another question for you all to consider." Then, hearing the sound of footsteps outside the room, he looked out of the window and then waved back at them. "Hang on a minute, my partner's looking for me."

Another detective—this one a young man earlier introduced as Jack West—appeared in the doorway. "Hey, Tom, I've checked out that stuff you asked about."

Detective Jenkins nodded at the younger man. "Yeah, so what'cha find out so far?"

The young man looked at a notepad. "We've confirmed the number of kidnappers as six. Four initially entered the church, with two remaining outside to secure the two ushers who were serving as parking lot attendants."

Detective Jenkins nodded. "And what about the vehicle? Anyone get the number of the van?"

Jack West shrugged. "Maybe."

"Kid, what do you mean, maybe?"

The younger man explained: "One of the children's teachers made a video of the van as it drove off. But the video resolution sucks and we can't make out the vehicle number. We're figuring that maybe the lab boys can enhance the image a bit . . . they're already scanning the place where the van parked for tire imprints . . . and one of the ushers said the van drove off east after leaving the church, so we're pulling in as much public CCTV footage as we can in that direction from traffic cameras and such."

Detective Jenkins looked pleased. "Well, that's a lot better than nothing. Any luck with fingerprints, Jack?"

"Nah, they all wore gloves." The young man checked his notepad one more time. "And, Tom, there one more thing."

"What's that?"

Jack West grinned. "Well, man, when I spoke to the church sound engineer, he told me he'd been recording the service so they could later make tapes from it, or maybe transcribe the pastor's message into a blog post. So, it turns out that he recorded everything the leader of the kidnappers said too. Audio from the service gets recorded onto a different hard drive from the one for the security system."

"Good, good," the older detective said. "One voice like that's definitely gonna help our identification and prosecuting once we catch 'em."

"Actually, Tom, there's two voices on the tape."

"Two?"

Jack West nodded. "Yeah, I listened to the recording. Mostly, it's the leader speaking, but at one point a woman tells him they've secured everywhere."

"Two's better than one," Detective Jenkins said, then nodded to Jack. "Okay, kid, you better head back to the auditorium now and keep an eye on stuff in there, while I round up talking to these guys. Once the officers' interviews with the church members are concluded they can all leave, but tell the sound engineers that we wanna talk to them personally." He looked back over at the church staff, who had been conversing in whispers. "What's the dude's name again?"

"Brother Mike," Frank Everett told him. "Mike Roscoe."

Detective Jenkins nodded and returned his attention to his young partner. "Yeah, Jack, tell Mike Roscoe and his assistants that we wanna talk to them, maybe we can figure out some other clues together."

The young man turned to leave, but then looked back in at Tom Jenkins. "Yeah and, man, the newsboys are here. They're asking if they can get a statement from you."

"Get rid of 'em for me, wilya. Tell them that we'll update them once we discover anything new."

The young man nodded and departed.

Detective Jenkins turned back to the church administrators. Frank Everett was seated again and Madge Fisher had stopped weeping. The detective walked back over to them.

"You all heard him," he said, nodding several times. "A little progress. And hopefully, we'll make a lot more in the coming hours. But I've got to advise you all to be careful when you talk to the press. This is gonna be big news for them, and they may hound you for days. Whatever you say, don't let them know that we suspect this to be an inside job. All that'll happen then is their informer will likely turn up dead on the roadside somewhere."

"Dead?" Josh looked horrified.

"Yeah, dead," the detective agreed. "From what you've told me of the sort of armory those guys were all carrying, they're not playing games. So, don't let on that we're on to them in that regard, yeah?"

"Yeah, sure," Josh said, with the others nodding their own agreement.

Detective Jenkins pulled up a chair and sat facing them. "Now, back to that question I was gonna ask you before Jack turned up. . . . Seeing as this is a church, I at first thought it wouldn't be a relevant course of inquiry to pursue. But, now that we've suspicions that this could be an inside job, I've got to know: did Pastor Fisher have any enemies?"

"Enemies?"

Madge Fisher looked horrified. "My husband was a very peaceful man! Everyone here loved him."

Detective Jenkins shrugged. "No offence, Mrs. Fisher, but I have to ask these questions. No one's universally loved. There's always gonna be someone with a grudge somewhere. And sometimes, focusing on those disgruntled individuals helps us narrow down our investigation."

He looked from Madge to Connie.

"I really have to agree with her," Connie said. "I also can't imagine anyone having any sort of quarrel with Pastor Fisher. He was such a calm and easygoing person."

"We've been at the church for three months now, and I can't recall the pastor raising his voice even once," Josh added.

"And that goes back at least two years for me," Frank said. "I'm sorry, detective, but this looks like a dead end. Just about everyone around here loves Pastor Fisher. I mean, he got along with everybody."

"Even with the Devil?"

Frank looked at the detective in confusion. "The Devil? What do you mean?"

Detective Jenkins shrugged. "Just a figure of speech. I'm merely restating my earlier point to Mrs. Fisher—that no one is universally loved. Reason this with me, folks—here we've got a peaceful man who's just been kidnapped. And if the kidnappers didn't abduct Pastor Fisher because of a grudge they've got with him, then why?"

"Maybe they want something," Josh said.

The detective nodded. "Yeah, kidnappers always want something. But in this case, what could that 'something' possibly be?" He looked out of the window, then back at the seated church workers. "I guess we'll just have to wait and find out what they want."

CHAPTER 3

Josh and Connie had spent most of the day giving interviews to reporters.

What had happened today was unprecedented in the little town of Wickenburg and everyone was still in shock.

Many of the parishioners were terrified. After a hurriedly convened prayer meeting to petition God for Pastor Fisher's safety and deliverance, Frank Everett had dispersed the church members, telling them to go straight home, not to panic, and that he would post all information about future church meetings on the church's online message board.

In addition to calming the congregation, there had also been the need to inform the Joy of Life church's state headquarters in Tucson of this monumental crisis before the news media did it for them.

Frank Everett had made the call; and this had resulted in Josh and Connie being put in charge of the Wickenburg church for now. There was no question of Madge Fisher acting as pastor until her husband was found. The woman was simply too distraught.

Finally, however, even the media newshounds had grown tired and had packed up their vans and driven off.

The officers and technicians from the Wickenburg Police Department had left shortly afterwards, after seemingly combing every inch of the church grounds for clues. The two detectives' interview with the sound engineers hadn't yielded much more than was already known.

"Alright, we've done what we can here for today," Detective Jenkins had told Josh before leaving, with Detective West nodding his agreement. "The lab boys are already working on enhancing that photo the lady took so we can get the van number from it." Then the lawman's expression grew really serious. "But remember, pastor, this is a kidnapping, so I expect that there'll soon be a communication with the church demanding a ransom of some kind. Only thing is, we've no way of knowing how long it'll be before they contact you. They may want to do it quick—now while you're still flustered, or they might let you sweat a bit, give you time to imagine the worst happening to Pastor Fisher so you'll be easier to manipulate." He scowled at Josh. "What I'm getting at here is, don't do anything without contacting the police, you hear me? Once they call you, you call us immediately."

Jack West nodded grimly and added: "If you let them call the shots, you just might get your pastor back in little pieces. Or not at all."

"Yeah, sure," Josh readily agreed. "I trust the Lord to give us His wisdom to handle this and get Pastor Fisher back again."

Detective Jenkins nodded, though his facial expression showed that he was wondering why the Lord had let the pastor get kidnapped in the first place.

Then the two lawmen strode off, got into their police cruiser, and drove away from there.

***

Finally, at around 7 p.m., Frank Everett left for home and Josh and Connie found themselves alone in Pastor Fisher's living room. Now that they were temporarily the church pastors, the couple intended to spend the night here in the parsonage. At the very least, they could keep an eye on Madge and be in the immediate vicinity should something come up.

Madge Fisher was in the house's master bedroom, sleeping under heavy sedation, with sister Juanita, who was a registered nurse, sitting beside her and keeping watch on her.

"Darling, could that female kidnapper have been Karen Houston?" Connie asked her husband after they'd eaten their dinner of takeout tacos, rice and beans ordered from Lydia's Lacanasta.

Josh shook his head. "No, honey, she definitely wasn't Karen." He paused for a few seconds, and then, counting off points on his fingers, explained his reasoning: "First off, she was too short, then she walked wrong, and of course her voice was completely different."

Connie nodded. "I didn't really think it was her either, but I wanted to hear your thoughts on it."

Josh smiled coldly. "I won't lie to you, honey. I would have loved for it to be Karen who'd been holding that gun. If she gets arrested for kidnapping Pastor Fisher, it will mean an end to her harassing the church."

"She hasn't harassed us for months now."

"Doesn't mean she's not planning to do so." He smiled at Connie again then released a long sigh. "Ah, it would have been so nice if she'd been the one. But no, the leader of the kidnappers clearly wasn't her brother Bill either. How unlucky can one be?"

Connie moved up beside him on the couch and placed her head on his chest. "Relax, honey, you're all worked up from everything. It's been a horrible day for everyone."

"Well, even if the Black Circle aren't behind this abduction, they're certain to get huge mileage out of it," Josh said. "Now everyone is going to be scared to attend our church services. And with good reason too."

"Yeah, God help us in this time of tribulations."

Josh had considered telling the detectives about the Joy of Life church's ongoing conflict with the Black Circle organization. But he'd decided to wait until he had definite proof of their involvement. What had happened here today was much more organized than back then when they'd tried to get him to shoot up the church in Tucson.

Josh and Connie turned on the TV. The abduction was headline news on all the local stations: ". . . This morning a gang of armed men burst into the Joy of Life Bible church in Wickenburg and kidnapped Pastor Amos Fisher during the Sunday morning service . . . the police are asking that anyone who has any information that might help solve this case should come forward . . . Amos Fisher had been pastor of the Wickenburg branch of the Joy of Life church for the past five years . . ."

Sister Juanita emerged from the bedroom.

"How is she?" Connie immediately asked her.

Sister Juanita, a short Mexican woman with long glossy hair, smiled and sat down. "Oh, she's alright. It's just the shock of things."

Connie sighed. "I know what you mean." She pointed to Josh. "I can't imagine what *my* reaction would be if it was my husband who got snatched like that." She pushed the single remaining takeout dinner on the coffee table towards sister Juanita. "This one's yours."

"Thanks," the nurse began eating.

Josh and Connie sat waiting for one of their cellphones to ring.

CHAPTER 4

The anticipated phone call didn't come that night.

Neither Josh nor Connie had slept well. Once sister Juanita had finished her meal the previous evening, Connie had suggested that they all pray and praise God for Pastor Fisher's safety. And this had been how they'd spent the time till midnight, when they'd retired to bed.

But now, at about nine a.m., when Josh was seated in the pastor's office trying to figure out whether or not to hold Tuesday's new convert's classes as usually scheduled, his phone rang. The number on the cellphone display was an unfamiliar one and Josh at first thought that it might be the kidnappers, but it turned out to be Detective Jenkins.

"Morning, detective."

"Morning, pastor. I got your phone number from Frank Everett."

"That's fine, any new developments?"

"Yes, I thought you might like to know that we've managed to enhance the license plate number for the kidnappers' van."

"Praise the Lord, that's great," Josh said.

"Not so great, I'm afraid," the detective said solemnly. "The van was reported stolen over in Amarillo, Texas a week ago. We ran a background check on the owner of the van, and guess what?" The detective laughed. "He's the pastor of the branch of your church over there."

Josh understood the lawman's mirth. "So, you're saying the kidnappers deliberately planned things to make us look foolish?"

Detective Jenkins's voice turned cold and businesslike again: "Sure looks that way to me, pastor. But there's still hope. We've pulled CCTV footage from several public locations along the way they drove after leaving the church; two of the videos show the van clearly enough. Looks like they were heading towards Phoenix, so we've alerted law enforcement officials over there to be on the lookout for the vehicle. Also, we're trying to track the pastor's cellphone, though that's so far proved a dud." He was silent for a while and then asked: "And speaking of phones, anyone contact you yet?"

"No one. I hardly got any sleep last night 'cos I kept waking up to check my phone, but no, we haven't heard from them yet."

"They'll call, you can count on that."

Once the detective had hung up, Josh left his office and went over to the parsonage to fill Connie in on the details of the phone call. When he was halfway there, she emerged from the parsonage and began hurrying in his direction with a worried look on her face. His first thought was that something bad had happened to Madge Fisher.

"Is everything alright?" Sister Juanita had had to go to work this morning and so Connie was taking care of the pastor's wife.

"The kidnappers sent a message."

Josh stared at Connie in surprise. "Sent a message? They didn't call?"

She shook her head. "No, they sent a video message to sister Madge's WhatsApp from her husband's phone."

She turned and, tugging Josh along by his shirtsleeve, hurried off towards the parsonage.

***

Madge Fisher was waiting for them in her living room. She was wrapped in a bathrobe and looked much calmer today, the result of another dose of sedatives this morning.

She pointed to her phone, which lay on top of the coffee table. "I didn't have the courage to keep watching it alone. What if they've harmed my Amos?"

Josh picked up the cellphone and handed it to the pastor's wife to enter her unlock code.

They replayed the video from the beginning. The video showed Pastor Fisher bound in a chair in a white room. The pastor looked okay, but was gagged with a dirty napkin.

"Oh, Amos!" Madge moaned like she was in agony. "Oh, darling! Lord Jesus help us!"

At first the person filming with the pastor's camera seemed to be having trouble making up his mind which angle was best to shoot from, because the image kept shrinking and expanding, at one point taking in the entirety of the abducted minister's body and then zooming in to show just his head.

But finally, the picture stabilized at a distance where they could see just Pastor Fisher's head and shoulders, with a lot of space above him. The reason for the gap above the pastor's head was revealed a few seconds later, when a stocky man in military garb and ski-mask (and whom Josh decided had to be the leader of the kidnappers) strolled into the picture and stood behind Pastor Fisher, with his hands resting on the pastor's shoulders.

"Hello, Mrs. Fisher," the man said, his deep and gruff voice instantly confirming him to indeed be the person who'd yesterday commandeered the church pulpit. "As you can see, because you obeyed our instructions yesterday not to hinder our escape by calling the police, your husband is still unharmed. But how long he remains this way is now entirely up to you and the others at the church."

"What on earth do they want from me?" Madge wept. "Oh, Lord Jesus, help me!"

The masked man laughed. "What we want from you Christian fools is for you to shut down the Joy of Life church in Wickenburg for good."

"What?" Josh and Connie both said in unison. "He can't be serious."

"Of course, you must be thinking I can't be serious," the kidnapper laughed as if reading their minds. "But I assure that I am dead serious." His right hand vanished behind the chair for a few moments, and when it reemerged it was clutching a large revolver, the muzzle of which he placed against the bound man's right temple, which made Pastor Fisher squirm with fear. "It's a simple exchange, folks: the end of your church in exchange for your pastor's life." He cocked the revolver by thumbing back its hammer. "The choice is of course, entirely yours."

On hearing this, Madge Fisher burst into fresh tears and slumped back on the couch.

Josh paused the video. "May the good Lord Almighty get us out of this mess," he said, glancing at Connie. "Honey, please fetch brother Frank. I need to call Detective Jenkins."

***

". . . You will sell the church property to the realtors Hunt and Adams," the masked man said in his gruff voice. "Once you've done so and we have confirmed the sale of the property, you'll have your pastor back safe and sound." He strode forward to the pastor's side and pointed his gun at the pastor's cheek. "Remember, you have just one week to do this. We're not playing games here."

Pastor Fisher was squirming against his bonds, with his eyes defiant. They could hear his loud mumbled protests.

His captor laughed and patted his head. "Of course, the good minister here doesn't want you to shut down the church. He would rather shed his blood for Christ; be a martyr for your Lord and savior. But I would advise you not to try any stupidity. We can always snatch someone else after killing dear Pastor Fisher here, maybe even you who are listening to us."

At this threat Madge Fisher emitted a loud moan of terror and slumped across the couch as if she'd fainted.

The ski-masked man laughed loudly. "That is all for now."

That was the end of the video, which this time they'd watched on a laptop that Detectives Jenkins and West had brought along with them. Once the video stopped playing, the two detectives looked grimly at those assembled in the parsonage with them, who were Josh, Connie, Madge and Frank.

"Well, they clearly mean business," Detective Jenkins said. "But on the positive side of things, at least they haven't harmed Pastor Fisher yet."

"We can't shut the church down," Josh protested. "That's simply inconceivable."

Jack West, the younger detective, nodded. "Of course not; we wouldn't expect you to. We'll have to try and stall them; drag things out until we can locate their hideout and rescue the pastor."

"Have you had any success so far with finding their van?" Frank Everett asked.

Detective Jenkins nodded. "Yeah, yeah, we've found it. I was about to call you concerning that when Pastor Josh called me. We found the van abandoned over in Glendale. Forensics have gone over it twice, but it's been wiped clean—not a single fingerprint they could use." He pointed to the frozen video on his laptop. "I think we'll have more success with this though. Not so much with the video, but . . . we'll trace the cellphone signal. WhatsApp conversations are encoded, but not who and where they come from."

Connie nodded. "But what do we do now? Like my husband already pointed out, we can't put the church up for sale. That's just impossible."

"If we give in to these demands then what's going to be next?" Frank Everett said. "We'll have given out clear signals that all these people need to do to shut down one of our branches is to kidnap someone."

Detective Jenkins shook his head. "No, you aren't gonna sell the church. But you've got to appear to want to do so." He smiled coldly. "They've already made one major mistake here."

"What do you mean?" Josh asked.

The detective explained: "They told you exactly who to sell the church to. Hunt and . . . " He looked at Detective West, who'd been mostly silent all this while. "What's their name again, Jack?"

"Hunt and Adams."

Detective Jenkins nodded. "Yeah. Hunt and Adams—I know that name, they're quite popular in the Phoenix area."

"You think they might be involved in this?" Josh asked.

"Nah," Jack West replied. "From what I recall of them, they're a hundred percent legit. Besides, they're too big—got way too much to lose by getting involved in something this scandalous, not to mention, paltry." He lifted a finger to make his point. "But what Tom's getting at is this—seeing as the kidnappers instructed that you sell your property to Hunt and Adams, we can stall the sale of the church by appearing to investigate those real estate guys. And besides, once we fill them in on the details, Hunt and Adams won't want to touch the church sale with a ten-yard pole, and that buys us some time to keep investigating."

"Yeah, that makes sense," Josh said, with Connie and Frank nodding their agreement.

"Please get my husband back alive and well!" Madge Fisher cried. "Oh, Lord Jesus, please, please, please, help me get Amos back alive and well!"

"Calm down, please," Connie said, hugging Madge. "God is in control of everything. The Devil is merely trying to ridicule the church." She looked over at Detectives Jenkins and West. "And I'm sure the police are doing everything they can to get Pastor Fisher back safe and sound."

Both detectives nodded and gave Connie and Madge reassuring smiles.

"That's right, ma'am, we are," Detective Jenkins said. "You see, it hasn't escaped my notice that this is the last surviving church in this town." He paused and looked puzzled. "Now, while I'm not a churchgoer myself, it has struck me as odd how all the churches here in Wickenburg have been closing down of recent. The scandals I could ignore—I'm a lawman; I've seen enough human behavior to expect the worst from people even at the best of times—but this . . . this all strikes me as indicating that there's something afoot in this little town of ours. Something *evil*." Now he really looked perturbed. "Or, why else do they want to shut this church down too? And, once we consider this to be the case, then I get the idea that some of the scandals which forced the other churches to close— remember how Rev. Philips kept insisting that he'd never seen that young woman before in his life—were frame-ups." He sighed. "Too late to do anything about all those others now. But, God helping me, I'll do my damnedest to prevent this church of yours from suffering the same fate."

"Thank you, detective," Josh said. "You've just brightened up our day."

"Rest assured we'll do our best." Detective West closed up the laptop they'd brought with them and began loading it into its bag. The two lawmen rose to their feet.

"Just one more thing," Detective Jenkins said before heading for the door. "We've got to keep a lid on this. Don't let the press get wind of what they're demanding."

"Yeah, sure," Josh said. "But what happens if they send a copy of their demands to the media too?"

"I don't think they will," Detective Jenkins replied. "I don't think these kidnappers—whoever their backing organization is—really want a public spectacle. Yeah, sure, they kidnapped your pastor in broad daylight. But, if my suspicions are correct and it's the same group responsible for shutting down the other churches here in Wickenburg, then they'll likely prefer that the Joy of Life church fade away quietly, just like the others did. Which means they won't court the possibility of the media putting two and two together like I just did and beginning to suspect and investigate a conspiracy."

"But wouldn't that be best for us?" Connie asked. "I mean to expose them?"

Detective Jenkins sat on the edge of the pastor's desk, then shrugged. "Maybe later, but not at this stage of things. Now, our primary focus must be on getting Pastor Fisher back alive and well." His expression turned very serious. "And also, there's another reason why I don't want news of this video spreading outside this room for the moment."

"Why's that, Tom?" This time it was Detective West who spoke.

"Because, Jack . . . remember what we discussed on our way here, about the Judas in the church?"

The younger lawman smirked and nodded, and the older detective returned his attention to Josh and the other church staff. "That's right, folks. We need to remember the spy in the church. Outside of the four of you in this room, we can't trust anyone else to not relay our conversations to the kidnappers."

Josh nodded. "I'd forgotten that the kidnappers had inside assistance."

"Yeah, so at the moment, everyone is suspect. Your sound engineer told Jack and I yesterday that not too many church members enter the sound booth . . . but it could be second-hand information that the kidnappers got. Unlikely for sure, but still possible." Detective Jenkins got up from the edge of the desk. "Well, that's it for now. Jack and I are gonna head back to the office and get this video the kidnapper sent you for analysis—maybe there's something forensics can determine from it. And we'll also run that trace on Mrs. Fisher's phone."

After the two detectives departed, the four church staff looked at one another.

"Let's pray," Frank Everett said. "At the moment my mind seems blank. It's bad enough that Pastor

Fisher was kidnapped but much worse to know that someone in our own church is helping the kidnappers."

Josh shook his head. "It's possible that that's not the case; you heard the detectives."

Frank shook his head and looked around at them. "I disagree. I don't know why this is, but I've got a deep witness in my spirit that we really do have a Judas amongst us—I don't mean here in this room—but . . ."

The four of them knelt on the floor and shut their eyes, and Frank led them in prayer: "Dear Heavenly Father, please help us in this time of need. Please help us find and rescue Your son and our pastor Amos Fisher . . ."

CHAPTER 5

The week passed quickly with few new developments.

Although Frank advised against it, Josh and Connie resumed church services.

"There's nothing else we can do," Josh explained to the worried church administrator. "If we stop holding meetings, it's as good as telling everyone that the Devil has won."

So, they had their regular new converts' class on Tuesday and the Bible study on Thursday. Ironically, both services were better attended than usual, the news of Pastor Fisher's kidnapping having sparked a sense of being persecuted amongst the small town's Christian community, so that now even those who hadn't been to church in years came to show their solidarity for the Joy of Life church.

"Don't give up hope," Josh told the congregation on Thursday. "There's no chance of our God failing us. Remember, that the Apostle Paul exhorts us to pray without ceasing."

Of course, neither Josh nor Connie could get over their fears that the kidnappers might return to stage a bloodbath against the worshippers.

But it didn't happen, and the week passed with a cloud of unease hovering over the little church.

A local political scandal caused press interest in the case to wane during the week, and those pressmen who still wanted 'exclusives' on Pastor Fisher's kidnapping shifted their focus from the church workers to the Wickenburg Police Department.

And also in the meantime, as a result of the police being short-staffed, Detective Jack West got transferred off the kidnapping case to investigate a brutal gang murder instead.

Detective Jenkins however continued to spearhead the police investigation into Amos Fisher's abduction, and he kept the church staff updated with all the latest developments in the search.

"Well, so far there's nothing to report," he told Josh and Madge Fisher via video conferencing on Tuesday morning. "I've been to Phoenix to see the realtors Hunt and Adams. Like I predicted, they totally deny any knowledge of the kidnappers, and I see no reason to doubt them."

Josh nodded at the image on the laptop, and the detective went on:

"Similarly, Mrs. Fisher, our trace on the video that was sent to your phone led nowhere, or rather it led to a small town in Nevada where the phone trail suddenly began looping in circles." He frowned. "We had to admit we were beat." He shrugged. "But we're still doing our best to find your husband, ma'am."

"I believe my Lord God that you'll find him soon," Madge Fisher replied him. "We've been praying non-stop here for his safe release."

Madge was much better now and able to function without medication. Now that she was past the initial shock of her husband's abduction, her disposition had become surprisingly calm and sunny.

"We need to keep an eye on her," Connie told Josh. "I think she's very close to a nervous breakdown. The last thing we need now is the pastor's wife going crazy."

"She seems okay to me. This is much better than her having hysterics."

Connie wasn't convinced, however. But there was little they could do. And she agreed that Josh was right: Madge functioning normally was much preferable to having to sedate her again.

***

On Saturday night Connie oversaw the prayer group meeting. As had been the pattern during this week's services, the church auditorium once more saw a higher attendance than was usual.

Oh, How I wish that this was the norm rather than the exception, Connie told herself, as she stepped up onto the altar to lead the intercessors. She'd left Josh on the phone, speaking to Pastor Micah Princeton, the pastor of the Joy of Life's Tucson branch, which was also the ministry's state headquarters. Pastor Micah wanted to come to Wickenburg tomorrow to attend the Sunday morning church service, but Josh had convinced him not to. Josh's argument was a simple one: What if you get kidnapped as well?

Apparently, most of the ministers at the Tucson church shared Josh's reasoning: One kidnapped pastor was enough. So, Pastor Princeton would remain at home.

"Okay, brothers and sisters," Connie told those assembled to pray. "We all know that there's only one thing uppermost in our minds at the moment and that's Pastor Fisher's freedom. So, let's pray to our Lord Jesus with all our might for our pastor's deliverance."

Everyone began praying. Connie put down the microphone and left the altar. She sat on one of the ministers' chairs and prayed hard, from the bottom of her soul.

But it soon became apparent to Connie Davies that this wasn't some ordinary prayer meeting she was overseeing. There was something different in the air tonight, beyond the usual sense of God's presence one expected in meetings of this kind. Yes, Connie did sense God's grace here in the auditorium with them, but she also sensed something else; and it took her a while to understand what that addition was:

Tonight, there was a special urgency about proceedings.

She looked around the auditorium. Some members were down on their knees at their pews, while other stood and spoke to the heavens. Yet others sat on the red carpeting in the aisles and at the front of the church, and other intercessors walked about the auditorium, lifting their hands and voices to God. But what was common to them all, what was unmistakable on their faces and in their voices, was the 'urgency'— a special burden to pray unlike any that Connie had witnessed in recent times.

It's almost as if we're praying not just for Pastor Fisher's release, but for the very life of this church.

As if the very survival of the Joy of Life church in this town depends on tonight's prayer meeting.

With this in mind, she climbed the altar and picked up the microphone once again. After tapping it several times to get everyone's attention, she said, "Brothers and sisters, I feel an intense burden to pray for the Christian ministry in this town—please add this to your prayers for the pastor's release."

There were nods all around. And when Connie left the pulpit again and the praying resumed, it felt to her as if they'd just plugged the building into a power station. The presence of God Almighty in the auditorium felt so real, oh so real.

And then suddenly Connie had a vision:

She was looking up through the roof of the church, which was suddenly transparent. And up there, perched on the ridge of the roof, sat a giant black bird. A huge and very horrible bird that was poised to tear the building to pieces with its claws and peck up the congregation as food.

In the vision Connie felt terrified; the bird was so big, so strong, so powerful—it seemed invulnerable. She also sensed the adversary's anger, an all-consuming rage against Jesus Christ and also against all those who worshipped him; this creature of Hell had only one desire and intention, and that was to completely annihilate Christians.

Connie reeled back before the threat it posed. Surely there was no way she and those with her in the church could resist this giant black bird.

And then suddenly she heard a voice from Heaven, saying, "Breakthrough. Breakthrough and victory in the name of Jesus Christ!"

And on that statement, a bolt of lightning came from Heaven and struck the giant evil bird. And then, cawing weakly, the huge bird toppled off of the church building and fell onto its back, where it kicked its legs a few times and then died. And once it was dead, its body crumbled down to a pile of feathers and ash.

Then the vision faded, and Connie realized what she'd just seen. And at the same time, she sensed a change in the atmosphere in the auditorium, a glorious shift in the tone of the intercessors' prayers. Where before the atmosphere had been a miserable and desperate one, a clutching at something one desired, now Connie sensed peace in the building. No one was praying as hard anymore; in fact, half of the congregation were now singing songs of praise and worship to the Lord.

Smiling, she returned to the altar.

"Okay, everyone, let's round up our prayers and come together again. I have a strong impression that Jesus has given us the breakthrough tonight. Does anyone else sense this?"

Half of the intercessors raised their hands in assent.

Connie told everyone the vision she'd had, then added, "So what we'll do now is, we'll just spend the rest of this meeting praising God." She looked at the clock hung on a support pillar opposite the altar. "We've about twenty minutes left. We're gonna spend all that time thanking our Lord for what he's done for us tonight, for this great victory that he's given us."

Sister Juanita raised a song and everyone else joined in:

"Thank the Lord God Almighty,

For he has given us victory over the Devil and his horde.

All glory be to Jesus . . ."

After the meeting had ended, sister Juanita called Connie aside. "I saw something like you did," she said. "A bird struck by an arrow through its heart. It fell and was unable to rise again."

"Praise God," Connie said. "I really believe now that the pastor will be released soon. Let's go and tell my husband the good news."

CHAPTER 6

Just like last week's, this week's Sunday morning service started normally again.

"I don't care what anyone says or thinks," Detective Jenkins had already informed Josh. "I'm not allowing a repeat of last week this week. I'm not saying they're gonna be foolish enough to come back here again, but then you never know."

So now there was a visible police presence at the church premises. Two police cruisers filled with heavily armed officers, most of them brought in from the nearby towns of Peoria and Glendale, were parked on either side of the building. In addition to this, two officers stood by the church gate, observing every vehicle that drove into the compound.

In addition to the police, two news vans were parked outside the gates, with reporters trying to interview those arriving for the service.

"Damn news vultures," Detective Jenkins had commented on his arrival here. "You'd almost think they want another kidnapping to occur."

Detective Jenkins was himself amongst the congregation, sitting in the back row so he could quickly respond to any emergencies.

Once more, the church was filled with people; this Sunday morning there were twice as many people in church as there had been last week.

"I just wish we didn't have this church growth because of a scandal," Connie whispered to her husband as her eyes scanned pew after pew filled with people she'd never seen before.

Josh nodded. He didn't understand why, but he felt very disturbed. Short of the kidnappers firing a rocket-propelled grenade at the church though, nothing could go wrong this morning. That much was clear, and yet, somewhere on the inside of him he felt disquieted.

He found his unease strange. He'd felt intense joy last night when his wife had told him her vision; what she'd seen had confirmed the feeling he'd gotten while praying earlier in the day: that God had given them a breakthrough. But since waking up this morning he'd been completely unable to set his mind at ease.

The choir and musicians came out of the choir room. A short while later, Madge Fisher came out of the vestry. Madge was preaching this morning.

"Yes, I want to do it," she'd insisted on Thursday when they'd been discussing the order of today's service. Madge had been scheduled to preach for a month now, but Josh had offered to substitute for her if she didn't feel up to it. "Both for myself and also to show the congregation that we're not being cowed by the Devil. Yes, Amos hasn't yet been returned to me, but I honestly believe that our Lord is in control of this situation and very shortly I'll reunited with my darling husband."

Now, Madge sat beside Josh and Connie. She wore a somber gray skirt suit and a black hat, and very pale lipstick. Her eyes were sad as she smiled at the young couple. "I feel very nervous," she admitted to them. "But I really need to get up on the altar and show the people that the Devil hasn't won yet; not by a long shot."

"We both understand," Connie said.

Josh looked around for brother Frank Everett, the church administrator. Frank wasn't in the church. But then he remembered that Frank was attending the service at the Joy of Life mother church in Tucson this morning, so that he could afterwards update the church leadership on the latest developments here in Wickenburg.

Well, at least they'll be delighted we're getting a full house again.

Sister Juanita, who had been sitting quietly behind Josh and Connie, got up and walked to the altar. "Brothers and sisters, let's all rise to our feet and prepare to welcome God's Holy Spirit into his temple . . ."

The people got to their feet and the service began. Josh still couldn't relax.

"You look worried," Connie said, as sister Juanita handed the microphone over to brother Paul, the worship team leader was to lead the praise session and then left the altar.

Josh leaned close and whispered in Connie's ear. "I keep getting a sense of déjà vu."

"Oh, honey, don't worry; try to relax. God's in control of the situation." Keeping her voice low so that Madge, who was seated on her immediate right, wouldn't hear her and start panicking, she added, "I don't see what could possibly go wrong this morning.

There are so many policemen here that it'd be suicidal for the kidnappers to try another abduction."

Josh tried to relax. "Yes, I know; but what about after the police leave? Tomorrow's the deadline the kidnappers gave us to sell the church; and so far, we've done nothing about it. What if they plan to snatch Magda or me later today . . . or worst still, you?"

Connie smiled at his statement of love for her. "Don't worry, darling, everything is going to be alright. Remember the vision I had last night—that God has given us the breakthrough. Now, let's try to concentrate on the service."

Josh *tried* to concentrate. He really, really did. But it was just impossible, because Josh had one particular worry that he'd not shared with his wife: *What if someone's sneaked a gun into the church service and is just waiting for the sermon to start before they start shooting everyone?*

With that uppermost in his mind, once the praise session ended and everyone was seated again, Josh began stealing glances around the church, looking for anyone who looked suspicious. He looked to the back of the church where Detective Jenkins was seated. The detective too was looking around at the congregation.

He's also suspicious that someone might have snuck a gun into the church!

But nothing happened, and finally, after the choir had sung their special number, Madge Fisher got up to preach the sermon.

There was a hush as Madge Fisher stepped up onto the altar and placed her bible on the pulpit.

She opened up her bible and smiled at the congregation.

"Brothers and sisters in Christ, I thank our God for the opportunity to be here and to address you all this morning," she said. "I know that many of you are very bothered by the abduction of my husband Amos Fisher. And yes, truly, it is a horrible thing, and a clear indication of the Last Days that our Lord and Savior predicted would come upon us. But please, brethren, we need to remember what the book of Psalms says . . ."

"I'm relieved that she's okay," Connie whispered to Josh. "I was scared that she was going to break down in tears on the altar. With those TV crews outside and all the reporters in here . . ."

Josh nodded back at her. "Yeah, you're right. Well, thank God that isn't happening."

"What are you looking around the church for?"

Josh sighed. He really couldn't tell Connie that he was scared someone might be in the church right now who was planning to shoot them. "I'm still nervous," he replied, not wanting to lie to her.

She giggled. "Take it easy, darling. Nothing bad will happen, you'll see. Try and concentrate on the message. If the congregation notice that you're worried, they're going to start feeling uneasy too."

Josh nodded. Connie was right. He really should set the church members a better example. So, after a final look back at Detective Jenkins and noticing that the lawman also appeared relaxed now, Josh focused his attention of what the pastor's wife was saying:

"And so, brethren, we must live for Heaven, not for this Earth. For what does it profit a man if he gains the whole world but loses his soul?" Madge was smiling at the audience and Josh realized he'd been wrong all along. There really was nothing to worry about. The niggling feeling of disquiet returned but he pushed it away.

Madge unclipped the microphone from its short stand and walked to the edge of the altar, where she leaned over as far as she dared and addressed her listeners. "So, folks, we must live for Heaven. We may feel—and yes, it is the natural thing to feel, that life is the most important thing there is—but thinking that way is simply evidence that we're not fully in tune with the Spirit of God. Like the Apostle Paul said . . ."

The congregation was eating the sermon up, hanging on every word that Madge spoke. They'd come expecting to see a defeated, wounded soldier of Christ, a woman who was facing the worst challenge of her years in the ministry, and instead they'd met a warrior who was clearly stating her faith in Jesus and declaring her refusal to be cowed by the abduction of the man she loved.

"And so, brothers and sisters, today I'm going to give you a personal demonstration of my dedication to our Lord. Our Lord said, 'I go to prepare a place for you,' . . . meaning he's gone to prepare a place for us. Brethren, I've no reason to doubt the words of our Savior. Have you any reason to doubt the Messiah?"

"No!" the congregation thundered.

Madge walked like a model along the edge of the altar. "I asked you a question, brothers and sisters in the Lord. Does anyone here have any reason to doubt what our Lord said in the Gospels?"

"No!" This time the noise was even louder.

Madge shouted it this time: "I'm gonna ask everyone here the same question one last time: Do you all believe that our Lord has really gone to Heaven to prepare a glorious place for we believers, those of us who are the children of God, those of us who are called by His most holy name!?"

"Yes, pastor, preach it!"

Madge waited and then laughed. "Then what are we all still doin' down here, people? I'd have thought that Heaven is where we all wanna be."

The congregation all burst into laughter, Josh and Connie and sister Juanita also. The laughter was so infectious that no one knew when the gun suddenly appeared in Madge Fisher's hand, or noticed where she'd pulled it out from.

But there it was all of a sudden—a shiny silver snub-nosed revolver that glittered in the lights over the altar. Madge held the gun in her right hand, having transferred the microphone to her left hand.

A sudden hush descended on the congregation as they realized what she was holding.

Oh, my God no, Josh thought. *I expected danger from every source . . . except the most obvious one.*

At the rear of the auditorium he saw Detective Jenkins squinting—seemingly unable to decide what Madge Fisher actually had in her right hand. Then the detective seemed to understand that Madge was holding a gun, because he got to his feet and started talking urgently into a walkie-talkie.

The silence in the church was so absolute now that you could have heard a pin drop. Several people had already ducked behind the pews, but, unable to resist knowing firsthand what was about to happen, were peeking over the top of those same pews.

Gun in right hand, microphone in left, Madge strutted across the limited space the altar provided. "Now, brothers and sisters, don't be afraid. I'm not gonna hurt any of you. But our Lord Jesus said we mustn't be afraid to lay down our lives for our faith. And so right now, I'll give you a public demonstration of what this really means!"

"No!" Josh gasped as Madge raised the snub-nosed revolver and placed it against her forehead. He cringed at the thought of what was about to happen, and yet despite his dread, saw no way to prevent the terrible occurrence.

"No!' Connie gasped, pressing herself against her husband as if she wanted to tunnel into his body to prevent herself from witnessing what seemed inevitable.

"No! Don't do it, Mrs. Fisher!" yelled Detective Jenkins as he ran at full speed towards the altar. "No! Stop!"

His words however fell of deaf ears.

Madge Fisher smiled at the stunned congregation. "Goodbye, brethren, I'm off to be with our Lord. See you all soonest," she said, and then pulled the trigger of the revolver.

Its sound caught by her microphone and amplified through the church's speakers, the gun shot seemed supremely loud in the auditorium. Madge's head jerked to the left as the bullet entered it from the right; and then it exploded outward in a shower of blood and brains that sprayed over the officiating ministers.

Madge wobbled in place for a second or two and then her body collapsed. She toppled over the edge of the altar and crashed to the floor, her shattered skull leaking a river of blood and chunks of brains onto the floor.

In the wake of Madge's suicide, the church fell completely silent. This was so unprecedented, so unexpected, that no one had the slightest idea of what to do or think. Several women in the congregation fainted. Most of the newsmen who'd joined the service were too confused to pick up their cameras or phones to try and capture the unique tragedy of the moment.

Detective Jenkins reached the front of the church and bent over the body, then, grimacing, he shook his head.

The detective looked up and his eyes met Josh's. Josh sighed in horror as he read the look on the other man's face. There was no need to call for an ambulance. But, even though he realized that the detective had had to make absolutely certain, considering the amount of blood that had splattered on himself and Connie, Josh figured that for everyone else in the building, Madge Fisher's death was a foregone conclusion.

When he could manage the words, Josh groaned to Connie, who was still pressed tightly against his chest, "Oh, no, I can't believe this is happening to us again."

Connie didn't reply. Josh turned to look at her. Connie wasn't moving. Josh was really scared when he couldn't rouse her—he thought a ricochet of the shot that had killed Madge had hit her.

It took Josh a few moments to realize that, like the women in the congregation, his wife had merely fainted from the shock and horror of what she'd just witnessed.

CHAPTER 7

Connie awoke slowly.

After spending a few moments getting her bearings, she remembered that she was lying in bed in one of the guest rooms of the church parsonage, where she'd been brought to lie down after she'd fainted in the auditorium. Sister Juanita was sitting beside her, reading a magazine.

"What . . . what . . ." Connie sputtered before the whole terrifying debacle came back to her. Madge Fisher preaching the sermon of her life . . . and then . . . then . . .

Sister Juanita had realized she'd woken up and was looking at her. "How in the world could we both have been so wrong?" she asked the Mexican woman. "I know what I saw, and you confirmed that the Lord showed you exactly the same thing. So, what went wrong?"

Connie stared intently at sister Juanita, expecting an answer of some sort, an explanation that would satisfy the pain now building inside her. "With what's just happened the kidnappers don't even need to demand that we shut down the church . . ."

"Shut down the church? What are you talking about, sister Connie?"

Connie realized she'd said too much. Although as far as she was concerned, sister Juanita was beyond reproach—it was impossible that her current companion could be the kidnapper's mole in the Joy of Life church—she recalled that Detectives Jenkins and West had mentioned the possibility of innocent church members unknowingly passing on sensitive information about the church to the kidnappers. And so, Connie reasoned, the less that sister Juanita knew about the actual state of things, the better for everyone.

"Nothing, sister," she told the nurse. "The pastor's missing, and now his wife just committed suicide on the altar. How many people do you think will be in the service on Tuesday?" Then before the woman could reply to that query, Connie had another, more urgent one: "Hey, where's my husband?"

Sister Juanita smiled. "Oh, he's with the cops."

Connie tried to get up. "I'd better go to him."

But sister Juanita gently pushed her back down onto the bed. "No. Pastor Josh asked me to keep you here. And I agree with him. Trust me, at the moment, you don't want to go outside into the church compound for any reason."

Connie didn't understand what she was talking about, until the other woman walked over to the bedroom window and pulled back the drapes just a little bit.

"Can you see the auditorium?" she enquired.

When Connie replied "No," sister Juanita drew the drapes back a bit more.

Connie gasped at the beehive of activity around the church. "Dammit, I forgot that the press were in the service. We've just made their day!"

Sister Juanita nodded sagely and shut the drapes again. "Oh, yeah, the press are having a field day alright. "The original two news crews quickly became six; and I've no idea how many newspaper journalists are out there at the moment; probably more than the members of our congregation."

"What time is it?"

Sister Juanita checked her wristwatch. "A few minutes to noon. You've been asleep for about an hour."

Connie nodded at the information. She felt strange; almost lost at sea.

"Sister Juanita," she called and then indicated the chair by her bedside.

Sister Juanita walked over and sat in the chair. "What is it, pastor?"

"I'm confused, I'm very confused," Connie said, with tears welling up in her eyes. "Why on earth would Madge Fisher kill herself? It isn't like her husband's dead, is it? We're doing what we can to get him back alive and . . ." She began crying, unable to stop herself. "Why, why, why? And at such a crucial time too. It's almost as if God is just watching us wallow in our misery. Almost as if he's enjoying this persecution we're passing through."

"No, no, pastor, don't say that," sister Juanita said quickly. "Remember that our Lord God works in mysterious ways, his wonders to perform."

Connie pushed herself up on her elbows. "That's the problem here. I don't see God's wonders. All I see is problem after problem after problem, day after day after day!" She looked defiantly at the other woman, daring her to counter her.

Sister Juanita stared thoughtfully at the floor for a few moments, then she looked back up at Connie and nodded. "I'm tempted to agree with you. But . . . but . . our Lord is never wrong. Last night during that prayer meeting, He showed us that He'd given us a breakthrough in this case of the kidnapping of Pastor Fisher."

Connie laughed coldly. "By killing his wife? How in the world is that any sort of a breakthrough? Yes, I know what I saw in that vision, and I've no doubts about it even now. But . . . the vision must have been related to something completely different. Because otherwise, you tell me, sister Juanita, exactly how does Mrs. Fisher killing herself on the altar in front of the biggest crowd that this church has seen in years count as a spiritual victory? Of course, it doesn't. All that's going to happen now is that we'll be in the news as a crank church that preaches how one can get to heaven through suicide. The enemies of the Gospel of our Lord are going to have a field day with this, aren't they?" Her eyes glared defiantly at sister Juanita. "Tell me, sister, aren't they?"

Sister Juanita had no reply to that.

Connie just felt tired. This whole thing was tiring her out.

Oh, dear Lord Jesus, she thought. *It would have been a whole lot better if Josh and I had never come to this stupid little desert town where nothing ever seems to go right for us.*

CHAPTER 8

A video taken by someone's cellphone showed the dead woman placing the gun to her head and smiling, then pulling the trigger.

". . . And yet another tragedy has struck the Joy of Life Bible Church in the town of Wickenburg." The newscaster was a blonde woman in a black suit. "This morning, the wife of the kidnapped head minister at the church committed suicide . . ."

The TV screen showed photos of Madge's corpse, which was thankfully covered with a sheet, but still had shockingly huge bloodstains at the position of her head.

Josh muted the TV and then stared morosely at Detective Jenkins. "Man, I don't know how long we can hold out after this."

Once more, the two men were seated in Pastor Fisher's office. There was some noise outside, but not much. All the congregation had gone home, traumatized by what they'd watched happen.

The reporters had tried to get interviews with Josh and Detective Jenkins, but both men had declined to comment. But their silence hadn't really mattered after all; at least three people had videoed the suicide on their phones, and the newshounds were more than happy with those recordings.

Detective Jenkins tapped his fingers on the pastor's desk. "You just keep praying to God, Pastor, while I'll keep investigating. All of this has got to break wide open at some point; and I suspect it'll do so soon."

Josh looked at him in surprise. "Are you suggesting that both mishaps are connected?"

The detective shook his head. "Not directly. Although, if the kidnappers had gotten a hold of Mrs. Fisher's psychological profile, they might have realized she'd do something like this." He sighed deeply. "But of course, I'm just speculating here. We don't know that she had any crazy in her before today."

Josh nodded. "She was just overwrought, that's all." Then he shook his head and pounded his fist hard on the arm of his chair. "But she was a *Christian,* sir. She was a Christian minister. She should know suicide is against God's laws." The preacher looked helplessly at the lawman. "Her faith in Christ should have been sufficient for her. It's not like it's the end of the world."

Detective Jenkins nodded. "No, it isn't the end of the world, Pastor. Hey, who's gonna handle the burial? I mean, do they have any kids?"

Josh nodded. "They've a son, Robert, a missionary in Thailand. His mother insisted that we didn't tell him his father had been kidnapped. But now . . ." he spread his hands in a defeated gesture, "we've no choice. I expect that he'll fly into the country sometime this week. As for the burial itself, Madge's corpse will have to remain in the funeral home until you find her husband. We can't bury her without him being present."

"Yeah, that's right, you can't," Detective Jenkins agreed and then got to his feet. "Well, that's about all we can do now. I'd suggest you go check on your wife now, while I go back to the station and see if there's any breakthrough in our search for the kidnappers."

Josh nodded weakly and also got up. The two men left the office together, and after shaking hands, walked off in different directions.

CHAPTER 9

Josh had so far been unable to contact the Fishers' son. This was possibly because Robert Fisher was out in some remote Thai village where cellphone communication was unreliable.

After trying his best to phone Robert, at noon on Monday Josh finally sent the young man both an email and a WhatsApp message asking him to get in touch quickly. He figured that if that didn't work, he'd try to get in touch with Robert's parent ministry, or ask the Joy of Life church in Tucson to handle the search for him.

But then, almost immediately after he had put down his cellphone, it beeped with a WhatsApp message alert.

Josh snatched the phone back up, thinking Robert had quickly replied him.

But it wasn't. This message had come from Pastor Fisher.

Pastor Fisher? How? Then he got it. *It's the kidnappers!* He opened up the message, saw the attached video, clicked on it to download and went looking for Connie, who along with church administrator Frank Everett, was sorting through files in one of the counseling rooms.

***

This video looked like it had been shot in the same room as the first one. Pastor Fisher was seated in the same chair, and was tied up the same way, but now he was naked from the waist upward. And that wasn't the only difference:

"Oh, my God, no!" Connie gasped on seeing that the pastor had been badly beaten, his chest puffy and purple with bruises, his cheeks swollen, his lips cracked and bleeding around the red ball-gag stuffed into his mouth. Pastor Fisher's eyes spoke of intense suffering, of intense pain. He was squirming against his bonds while the person operating the phone camera once more attempted to get his picture focus right.

"How could they do this to him?" Connie asked the two men in a horrified voice.

Josh shushed her. The leader of the kidnappers had entered the picture. The ski-masked man strode back and forth across the foreground several times and then stopped and pointed a finger at the camera.

"You fools don't get it, do you? You think this is a joke?" He stepped back until he was standing on the right side of his bound captive, and pointed to the bruises on the man's skin, starting from his belly, which was completely discolored with dark swellings, and slowly moving upwards until he reached the man's head, which he gripped in both hands and forced forwards towards the camera. "Does this look like a joke to you!?"

He gripped Pastor Fisher's ears and twisted them both hard, until tears appeared in the man's eyes. "I don't think you realize how serious we are about you shutting down that pig sty you call a house of worship."

"I wish we could call them," Frank, who had a pained look on his face because of how his boss was being manhandled, said. "We could try to negotiate with them."

"The cops already tried calling them," Josh said. "But apparently they aren't really sending this video from the pastor's phone, but from some dark web server which can't be traced."

In the video, the kidnapper was still twisting the pastor's ears. But now he stopped doing this and laughed loudly.

"First of all, I must extend my condolences to you all concerning Madge's amusing death. No, who am I kidding?—that silly woman won't be missed by me. Good riddance to bad rubbish." He tapped the pastor's head. "But you still have one of these idiots left that you can save." The kidnapper now either leaned forward or the man filming moved the camera in close because suddenly the ski-masked head filled the camera frame. Now his voice was loud, almost a shout: "Now, listen to me, the lot of you stupid Christians in that stupid church of yours. "I'm giving you one more week to do this. Just one week. Shut that church down and sell it to whomever will buy it. Highest or lowest bidder? That's up to you, just so long as you're out of there by next Sunday." The magnification reversed again, until the captive was also in the picture; and they saw that the kidnapper's chest was heaving as if he was caught up in a great frenzy of emotion.

"And now, just so you don't think I'm fooling around . . ."

"No, no, no!" Connie gasped as the knife appeared in the kidnapper's hand.

Laughing like a maniac, the evil man pulled Pastor Fisher's right ear out from his head and began cutting it off.

Josh just managed to grab hold of Connie before she fainted again.

"Oh, my God, what on earth is wrong with these people?" Frank Everett gasped in a horrified voice.

CHAPTER 10

The rest of that afternoon was taken up with meetings, both physical and online.

First off (after Connie had been carried off to the parsonage and laid in bed), Josh forwarded the video to Detective Jenkins. Then he also sent a copy to Pastor Princeton at the church's Tucson branch. Then, after arranging to meet with the detective in an hour, he and Frank Everett held a video conference with the ministers over in Tucson.

"We're going to pretend to sell the church," Frank said after the video conference ended.

"Pastor Princeton is vehemently opposed to us doing so," Josh said. "You just heard him. He's completely against anything that even hints of capitulation to the demands of Satan's followers."

"That was all for show," Frank explained. "Remember that I was over at the Tucson church yesterday, while all the madness was happening here." He waited till Josh nodded that he remembered, and then went on: "Well, while I was there Pastor Princeton called aside into one of the counselling rooms and told me he figured we should pretend to shut down the church. He didn't want to mention it in the general meeting we had with the other ministers because of our suspicions that the kidnappers have inside help. And that's the same reason he now didn't say anything either."

"But who do we pretend to sell it to?" Josh asked. "Yes, I agree that it's a great way to secure the pastor's release, but if we're going to do it, it has to seem real." A vivid memory of the kidnapper's knife slicing into Amos Fisher's ear flashed before his eyes and he grimaced and felt like puking. "I'm not looking forward to us receiving any of the pastor's body parts by courier."

"No problem there," Frank said. "Last night Pastor Princeton sent me a list of three Christian realtors we can contact to handle the deal. He's already filled them in on what's going on; we just have to set things up."

Connie opened the office door then and walked in. Josh was relieved; she looked much better, though her eyes were red and puffy.

"Did I miss anything?" she asked, rubbing the back of her neck. "I'm sorry I fainted again, but . . . but seeing that . . ."

"You've nothing to apologize for, sister," Frank Everett said. "I took all my willpower not to throw up."

Connie kissed Josh and sat down beside him. "So, what's new?" she asked.

"We're off to the Wickenburg police station," Josh explained. "Do you feel up to coming along?"

"Yeah, sure," Connie said. "So long as I don't have to watch that sickening video again."

Josh spent the trip to the offices of the Wickenburg Police Department under a mental cloud. Something was wrong in all this. A kidnapping. A suicide. Torture. What was the connection?

"Yeah, pretending to sell the church is a good plan," Detective Jenkins agreed when they were alone with him in his office. "It buys us investigators some good time."

"Any new developments in your search for Pastor Fisher?"

The lawman shook his head. "Still can't find anything. We're once more trying to trace the pastor's cellphone, but so far, nothing. The trail leads out to the same desert town and loops around in circles like last time." He paused and frowned. "Oh, and I almost forgot: just to keep you informed of things, Mrs. Fisher's autopsy is scheduled for tomorrow morning. It isn't like they'll find anything suspicious— everyone in the state of Arizona knows how she died—but considering what's currently going on with the church, we gotta have it done for records purposes."

"I understand," Connie said. "I still can't clear the images of yesterday morning our of my head. And now this horrible video this afternoon . . . what is the world coming to?"

She stared plaintively at the detective as if she was going to cry, and he had no idea whatsoever of what to say to comfort her, so he was relieved when her husband pulled her close to him and said comfortingly, "These are the End Times, honey. Remember, the Apostle Paul warned us that in these last days perilous times would come. Unfortunately for us, His prophecy is being fulfilled right in our neighborhood."

Frank Everett frowned. "My worry now is that the kidnappers might still kill Pastor Fisher even if we appear to comply with their demands. It's really a lose-lose situation for us."

"I see what you mean," Detective Jenkins said. "But it's our best option now." He smiled grimly. "You just gotta pray that we get a break soon, and that we can flush out these perpetuators before they have a chance to kill him."

Connie nodded. "Yeah, at the moment praying is all we can do."

Detective Jenkins looked at Josh. "Any luck with contacting their son yet?"

Josh shook his head. "None. But in a way that's a blessing. None of us wants to be the one to tell him what's happened here."

As Frank drove them back to the church, Connie said, "The prayer group is holding an emergency meeting tonight. We're all perplexed at how things went so awry after Saturday's meeting. You guys could join us if you like."

"Sure, why not?" Josh said. "How 'bout you, brother Frank?"

"I'd love to, but I can't," Frank said. "My mother-in-law's in town and she thinks I'm doing my best to avoid her." He glanced back at Connie. "She's right of course, but my wife insists I have dinner with everyone tonight."

They all laughed at that, a brief comic respite amidst the darkness that seemed to be settling more and more over them with each passing hour.

CHAPTER 11

The prayer meeting that night was a time of intense and violent prayer . . . of pushing up against the gates of Hell . . . of binding and loosing . . . of crying to God for favor and deliverance. Neither Josh nor Connie had been in a prayer meeting like this one before. And when it was over, everyone was worn out. You could see it on their faces; that tonight they'd used up all their personal spiritual resources beseeching God.

Connie saw no visions this time, nor did she desire to. She still hadn't gotten over the fallout from the last one. But still, she had the feeling that they'd gained another huge breakthrough tonight; that they'd pushed the forces of Darkness to their limits and that those forces had crumbled like paper bricks.

Feeling as winded as if she'd run a race, Connie staggered up to the microphone and told the intercessors: "Well, everyone, we definitely *know* God heard us tonight. So, go home, go to bed, and remember to thank God for the victory."

"I can't shake the feeling that we're right on the verge of victory," Josh told Connie while the church members dispersed. "Something definitely changed tonight."

Connie nodded. "Yes, I felt it too. I didn't tell the intercessors 'cos I didn't want to raise anyone's hopes. It'd be cruel to do so, knowing that tomorrow you're going to put up a 'For Sale' sign on the church."

CHAPTER 12

The next day, however, Josh found that he couldn't start the job of selling the Joy of Life church premises.

He'd pick up his cellphone to call one of the three realtor companies that Pastor Princeton had suggested to them, open up the list of names and contact numbers, and then, suddenly not feeling ready to start the conversation, would close the message with the contact info again and put the phone back down on the desk.

One time he even got so far as making the call, but immediately cut it off.

What's wrong with me? he wondered. It wasn't as if there was any awkwardness involved in the process. The men he was calling all knew that the church sale was a sham. The only reason he'd been given three numbers was in case the kidnappers were tapping his cellphone line—which was quite possible since yesterday's gruesome video had been sent directly to him. He was supposed to discuss with each realtor's representative and then supposedly choose the one he felt the most confidence in; it didn't matter which of them it was. Then, once the wheels of the sale had supposedly been set in motion, he, Connie and Frank would wait to see what the kidnappers would say and do.

But no, Josh was simply unable to call any of the three realtor companies.

"How far've you got with it?" Connie asked when she brought him coffee at 11 a.m.

"I haven't even begun," Josh said. He smiled ruefully at her look of surprise and then explained to her what had been happening.

"And now that I'm telling you about it," he said. "I have the feeling that we're being really premature about this. Selling the church, I mean."

"It's a *fake* sale, honey," Connie corrected him. "And I don't see how we're possibly being premature." Then she looked worried and looked cautiously around the missing pastor's office. "Oops, maybe I shouldn't have said that in here. It's just occurred to me that in this case the walls may literally have ears. Brother Frank's Judas may not be one of the church members at all but instead a recording device—or several of them—planted around the church."

Josh scowled at her suggestion. "Well, it's too late for that now, honey. And besides, I don't think that's the case. Not that someone couldn't have easily planted a bug in here all this while, but that we've had so many meetings in here discussing the case—both with the police and with others—that if we are being bugged, the kidnappers should have a good knowledge of our plans." He paused to take a sip of his coffee and then looked moodily at his wife, with the weight of the crisis etched in every inch of his handsome face. "But judging from their most recent correspondence with us—I mean the video, honey," he explained when she gave him an enquiring look, "they don't seem to know what we're up to any more than we know where they're doing."

He drank more coffee while Connie nodded. "Yes, darling, I guess you're right."

"Where's brother Frank?" Josh asked. "I know it seems like we're doing it quite a lot nowadays, but I really feel like we should pray some more about this. In fact, I feel a heavy burden to pray right now."

Connie shrugged. "Brother Frank had to go drive his mother-in-law to the airport in Phoenix. I told him it was okay."

Josh shrugged. "Looks like it's just you and I doing the praying then."

Connie nodded. "You're the best prayer partner any woman could ever wish for."

Josh grinned at the compliment, finished his coffee, and opened up his Bible.

"The scripture says here in First Thessalonians chapter five verse seventeen: 'Pray without ceasing.' "

They shut their eyes and Josh prayed:

"Heavenly Father, Lord of all creation, please help and guide us at this time . . ."

After praying to God for a quarter of an hour, Connie said. "Darling, I have a witness in my spirit that we should search the parsonage. I strongly feel that either among the pastor's or sister Madge's belonging, we're going to find something to help us resolve this matter."

Josh nodded. He had exactly the same spiritual witness as his wife did. "Yes, let's head over there right away. It's just occurred to me that Pastor

Fisher's kidnapper—I mean, their boss—might be a close friend of his and that we'll find a clue to his identity in the house. Maybe an address book or something."

"Should we call Detective Jenkins?" Connie asked.

Josh shook his head. "Too early. We'll wait until we find something of interest. That way, if we don't discover anything special, we won't have wasted the detective's precious time."

"Okay," Connie agreed. "May God guide us in our search."

***

They stepped outside. Looking around the church compound, Josh felt a sinking feeling in the pit of his stomach. The entire premises already had the look of an abandoned lot to it. The only car out in the parking lot was his and Connie's. And none of the congregation were in sight. Even Randy Bullswirth, the new church gardener and handyman, wasn't visible.

Staring at this place you'd think that the Devil has already won the war, Josh thought grimly, his hand automatically detaching from Connie's grasp and sneaking around her body to pull her close to him as they stood watching.

"I've never felt so exposed and alone in my life," Connie said with a shiver, echoing his exact thoughts.

"Our Lord's little finger is greater than Satan's entire army combined," Josh said. "Come on, honey, don't be discouraged. Let's go search the parsonage."

Connie nodded and they walked around the nearer end of the administration block.

CHAPTER 13

Although it only possessed a ground floor, the church parsonage was a large building. It had four bedrooms with two bathrooms, a huge kitchen, a study and a separate library.

"Where do we begin?" Josh asked after unlocking the front door and stepping inside

"I dunno," Connie said, following him through the door. "Now that we're in here, there seems to be nothing to look for. We've both slept here and this place is just an ordinary house." Her gaze fell on a picture of Madge Fisher and tears came to her eyes. "Why would you go and kill yourself?" she silently asked the portrait so her husband wouldn't hear her.

Josh walked over to the bookcase on the far side of the living room and began dislodging its array of Bible reference texts. "Just look through everything— we want anything unusual." Then he corrected himself. "No, not unusual stuff, just anything that might give us a line on the kidnappers' identities."

***

Connie nodded and walked past him, down the hallway and into the couple's bedroom. She stood for a minute at the foot of the bed looking around, then walked to the nearer of the two nightstands and pulled out both of its drawers. Books, a penlight, old credit cards, eye drops, an old pair of reading glasses. Connie smiled on seeing the glasses. Madge didn't wear glasses so this must be the pastor's side of the bed.

She shut the drawers again and walked around to the other nightstand. Old Christian tracts, a powder compact . . . the bottom drawer contained folded underwear and an old cellphone that refused to power up.

Sighing, Connie left that nightstand too and walked over to the closet.

***

Josh searched everywhere in the living room. Seeing as the pastor had been abducted during the church service, the police had had no reason to search the parsonage for clues; they had just asked for whatever info they'd needed.

The bookcase provided no clues—it was just lots of Bible concordances, lexicons and maps; everything in short which Pastor Fisher hadn't had space for in his library. Josh intended to go through the library next, but he'd figured that seeing as the living room was where most socializing occurred, it was possible that something might be discarded here by accident, or simply shoved in between the book volumes to be retrieved later.

After searching the bookcase, Josh began flipping the chairs over to see if anything had fallen beneath them. And it was while doing this that he felt a resurgence of that earlier sense of impending discovery, the feeling that something relevant to the kidnapping was hidden in this house, if only he and Connie knew where to look for it.

After wondering if he'd need Connie's assistance, Josh managed to flip the heavy couch over onto its back. Once this was done, he sat down for a few seconds to catch his breath before reversing the flipping process so as to replace the couch in its original position. But then his attention was caught by something silver lying on the rug, near one of the couch's rear legs.

He got up and walked over to it, picked it up and stared at it.

It was just a cross on a chain, possibly forgotten by a visitor to the house at some point.

Josh was about to put the cross into his pocket when he realized that, judging from the position of the chain, the cross was actually upside-down.

A Satanist cross? I think this is the breakthrough we're looking for. Who could have left this here?

It was then than he heard Connie yelling his name. "Hey, darling, come in here! Come in here right now!"

The urgency in her voice was compelling. Josh left the overturned couch where it was and hurried down the hallway to the Fishers' master bedroom.

***

Searching the closet, Connie had first of all gone through the pockets of each of the pastor's suits. It would be easy for him to forget a business card belonging to some acquaintance in one of them, and maybe said acquaintance held the key to this mystery.

But she hadn't found anything in his pockets. So, sighing in disappointment, she'd turned her attention to the boxes of shoes at the bottom of the closet. She hadn't yet checked Madge's things. She was presently examining the left side of the closet and the late pastor's wife's clothes were arranged on its right side, lots of hanging pantsuits and skirt suits and several shelves' worth of handbags, not to mention jewelry boxes.

Connie had picked up the shoe boxes from the bottom of the closet and then she'd heard a soft 'click' sound.

She'd looked back into the closet, not at first understanding that by lifting one of the shoeboxes she'd activated a hidden switch in the floor of the closet. She had still been trying to work out what had made the strange clicking sound when the rear of the closet had slid aside to reveal a hidden room behind it.

Connie had felt around inside the closet until she found a hidden light switch and clicked it on. Then she'd leaned forward and peeked into the concealed space.

She saw that she'd unveiled a hidden stairway that led downward to an underground room.

Her curiosity overriding her alarm, Connie had stepped through the opening and had descended halfway down the stairs, where she'd paused and looked around.

The hidden basement seemed to be a library. It was a large room with two huge bookcases, a large reading desk with two laptops on it, and several comfortable chairs.

But the hidden room also contained many other objects that made Connie's eyes and mouth gape open in disbelief.

That was when she'd begun yelling for Josh to come.

CHAPTER 14

"Oh, my God," Josh said when he'd joined Connie down in the basement room.

Josh felt as confused as his wife by all the occultism on display. The room's crimson wallpaper was patterned with black pentagrams; each wall of the room had a large metal upside-down cross positioned right in its middle; and two large brass sculptures of the Devil stood in opposite corners of the room, both with obscene leers on their faces. Shelves on the walls held all sorts of occult paraphernalia, from colored potions in bottles and jars of preserved animal parts to human skulls and strangely warped knives and chalices. All the books in the bookcases had something to do with magic and devil worship of one kind or another.

"Darling, I think Pastor Fisher and Madge were actually devil worshippers," Connie said in a subdued and horrified voice.

"Yeah," Josh reluctantly agreed. "It seems impossible to me that such could be the case, but how can one deny all this evidence right in front of us?"

Josh felt very frightened being in here, but with Connie gripping his arm and following him, he walked forward to one of the laptops on the reading desk. He pulled two chairs up to the desk, sat in the right hand one and powered up the laptop.

"Are you sure we shouldn't let the police come and handle this?" Connie asked nervously. "Being near all this devil-worship stuff scares me."

Josh shook his head. "Not yet, honey. We still haven't solved the mystery of who kidnapped Pastor Fisher."

Connie sat in the second chair. "I think it's obvious that he faked his own kidnapping. That's how it looks to me."

The laptop had powered up without requiring a password. Its desktop background was a pentagram with a stylized goat's head motif.

Josh had been about clicking on the Firefox internet icon, but on hearing what Connie said, he paused and stared at her in shock. "What?"

She nodded back at him. "Yes, to my mind that's the most logical assumption. I think Pastor and Madge Fisher are members of"—she stopped speaking and, placing her finger on the laptop's touchpad, moved its cursor over onto the desktop goat's left eye.

"What are you doing?" Josh asked.

"Just watch," Connie said, clicking twice on the goat's face. "And this isn't an eye—there's an icon of a black circle overlaid on it."

Josh realized that she was right: there *was* a black circle overlaid on the goat's left eye.

The desktop background now altered to a black window with an inset red rectangle for text input. "Welcome to the Black Circle," read large words at the top of the screen. "Please enter your password."

"See?" Connie said in disgust. "It's our old friends the Black Circle again." She looked pointedly at her husband. "So, it's clear to me that all this while Pastor Fisher and Madge have been working with them to try to shut the church down. They're the Judases."

"But why are they so insistent on shutting every church in Wickenburg down?" Josh pondered aloud. "What's so important about this little town? Tucson has five or ten churches for each one Wickenburg had and they're all still standing."

Connie shrugged. "Beats me. But please, darling, let's go back upstairs. All I want now is to leave this creepy basement." She gestured about helplessly at the basement's occult-themed wallpaper and the pair of brass Devils in its corners and then stared pointedly at Josh. "Or what are we gonna do now? Try to crack their password?"

He shook his head. "No, there's no point; and besides, just being down here with all this disgusting stuff is making me feel sick too. Let's just head upstairs and call Detective Jenkins. And then we'll call the mother church in Tucson and tell them what we've—"

"Not so fast," a familiar voice said from behind them.

"What?" They both spun around. "Pastor Fisher?"

It was and yet wasn't Pastor Fisher.

"Just a projection of myself," the missing man explained with an evil leer. "I'm quite far away from here at the moment."

"How could you do this to us?" Connie asked angrily.

This version of Pastor Fisher was semitransparent, like he was there and yet not there. And there was a darkness to him that extended far beyond the somber tones of his image; a darkness that appeared to radiate from the core of his being. He was dressed in a magical surplice, in this case a black wizard's robe with a hood that obscured all of him except his face, his hands and his feet.

Staring at the man was disconcerting to say the least.

"Hello, you two fools," Pastor Fisher said, an uncharacteristic smirk on his face. "It's very unfortunate that you've discovered Madge and I's little secret."

Josh managed to get over his shock. He gestured around at the satanic objects in the room. "You call *this* a 'little' secret? You're a Devil worshipper!"

The ghostly Pastor Fisher laughed. "Yes, I am, and I have been all of my life. Madge too, we both hate your Jesus with every fiber of our being."

"So why join the Christian ministry then?" Connie asked. "Why pretend for all these years?"

"A necessary sacrifice to prove my dedication to our cause. As a Christian minister I was able to do much wickedness to the church; and no one would ever suspect me of it; no, the faithful and humble pastor Amos Fisher has always been above reproach." He pointed towards the powered-up laptop, which was still requesting a password. "The Black Circle have rewarded me well—I have no regrets."

"So, you planned your own kidnapping to force us to shut down the church?" Connie asked.

"Yes," the hooded specter confirmed. "And it has worked too. Just a little bit more pressure and you fools will capitulate, and this town will be completely ours."

Josh now had confirmation that the Black Circle were responsible for shutting down the other ministries in Wickenburg.

"So, sister Madge's suicide is a part of this too?" he asked. "She didn't kill herself just because she was distraught?"

Pastor Fisher laughed and gestured left and right at the occult items in the basement, at the bookcases with their evil books and the shelves with their jars of repulsive content. "Distraught? Madge? Hahaha! That is the funniest thing I've ever heard." Then the smile vanished from his lips and his gaze turned Arctic cold. "No, Madge *wanted* to die. She was tired of this silly Christian masquerade and wanted to join our lord Lucifer in Hell. And so she decided to exit this world in a manner that would shame the Church, her hated enemy."

"But why?" Connie asked. "Why are you—the Black Circle—so intent on shutting down all the Christian ministries in Wickenburg? Why is this small town so important to you?"

"We, the Black Circle, have a grand plan," Pastor Fisher began. "This town . . ." Then he laughed softly. "No, there is no point in telling you two what we intend to do. Both of you will soon be dead anyway. I will let your uncertainty about our plans haunt your last minutes."

"Dead? What are you talking about?" Connie stared at him like he was insane. She found it very disconcerting, how, if she turned her head sideways just a little, she could practically see through his body.

Pastor Fisher laughed. "This is the last stage of our plan—to rid the Earth of you two. Originally, your deaths were supposed to have occurred up in the church auditorium, but now . . . if you die down here in the basement, it makes little difference to us." He gestured around at the shelves and the statues of the Devil. "And when you're dead, none of these glorious tributes to my master Satan will be found down here. This land will be considered to be cursed by God and abandoned by all. And finally, Christianity will have been purged from Wickenburg."

"Forget it," Josh said. "We're under the protection of the blood of Jesus; we're not about to die to please your silly organization."

"No, we're not!" Connie fiercely agreed. "We're under God's protection."

"Oh, are you? We'll see about that!" Pastor Fisher angrily muttered some guttural words and the basement's stone walls began shaking.

And then, while Josh and Connie watched in shock, both Amos Fisher and the single exit to the basement vanished.

"What?" Josh gaped at Connie as plaster flaked away from the ceiling and gaping cracks in the wall tore through the satanic wallpaper.

A loud wrenching noise overhead forced them to look up. A huge crack had appeared in the stone ceiling. Josh pulled Connie out of the way as large chunks of concrete began raining down. There was another wrenching noise and the steel supports in the basement ceiling began snapping all along its junction with the walls.

"We'll be killed if the ceiling falls on us!" Connie said.

Josh dashed across the basement to where its door had been and desperately ran his fingers over the wall there, hoping the door's disappearance was merely an illusion. But this was no illusion; that area of the basement wall was smooth concrete now, unpainted and without wallpaper.

More concrete chunks fell from the ceiling and the walls cracked and bulged inward. Plaster dust filled the air.

Another wrenching noise made them realize that the stone ceiling seemed about to rip loose of its moorings and fall on them. Visibility in the basement was now severely limited by the dust everywhere. Both Josh and Connie were already covered in dust and both were coughing.

Josh looked around. "Quick, let's get under the desk! It'll shield us a little when the ceiling comes down!"

Her eyes wide with fright, Connie nodded.

But then Josh heard the still small voice of the Holy Spirit say: "Pray for God's help and salvation."

Josh's eyes widened. He realized that in their panic over what seemed like certain death down here they'd both completely forgotten to ask for God's assistance in this dilemma.

He pulled Connie away from the desk which she'd been about to duck under. "Oh, God please save me and my wife now, in Jesus's name. Don't let us die down here, oh Lord. In Jesus's name!"

"Amen!" Connie shrieked.

The ceiling shook mightily one final time and rained down plaster on them and a mighty cloud of dust. Then as the dust settled, Josh and Connie made out a huge figure standing there in the basement with them.

Their initial fear that Pastor Fisher had come back vanished when they realized that the huge figure was holding up the trembling ceiling with one hand.

They gaped at each other and then back at the angel. Sure, they'd expected God to intervene in this situation, but not as miraculously as this!

The angel was dressed in white and gold clothes; his hair was black and his skin the color of bronze and his eyes glittered. His head almost reached the basement ceiling. He smiled down at them.

"I am sent from the presence of Almighty God to get you out of here," he said in a gentle voice that immediately calmed their fears. "This whole building is going to collapse to rubble but I must first rescue you before it happens."

Josh nodded. "Thanks." Then he gestured at the basement wall. "But . . . but there's no door anymore."

Still smiling, the angel gestured to Josh to move out of the way. Then, after stepping closer to the wall (and with his other hand still holding up the ceiling), the angel punched the wall with his free hand.

The stone wall shattered as if it was made of paper. Chunks of wall crumbled like powder, revealing the stairway behind.

"Go quickly now," the angel told them. "You will make it outside safely and then this whole building will collapse."

Josh grabbed hold of Connie's hand and together they fled up the steps.

Once upstairs they understood what the angel had meant: the entire building was falling in on itself, with stone and plaster crumbing from the walls and ceiling. As they emerged from the basement, a roof support beam fell through the ceiling and crashed into the Fishers' bed.

"Go, go, go!" Josh yelled at Connie, shoving her ahead of him out into the hallway.

They ran out through the living room, which was a scene of pure chaos, with glass scattered about from shattered windows and the ceiling almost completely fallen in on itself.

Then they were at the front door. Josh got the door open and pushed Connie outside in front of him. They set off running for the church's admin building.

"Don't stop! Keep running!" he yelled to her when she slowed down, pulling her after him until they'd reached the safety of the administration block.

Only then did he dare turn around and stare at the parsonage.

Just like God's angel had told them, the parsonage was crumbling, with its roof collapsing inward as if something had crashed down on it and the walls breaking apart as if an invisible wrecking ball was at work.

"I-I have the f-f-feeling that this is wha-wha-what it looked like wh-wh-when the walls of Jericho f-f-ffell d-d-down," Connie wheezed through gasps of breath. "I-I-It's just c-c-crazy."

Josh hugged her and nodded. He was very relieved that they'd escaped alive from the chaos.

"Glory to our Lord God for sending His angel to save us," he said.

"Yes, yes, yes!" Connie wept. "All glory to the Lord God on high!"

The parsonage continued coming apart. Now, a huge cloud of dust filled the air over the spot as the building crumbled to the ground. On the highway that ran alongside the church compound motorists had begun stopping to view the strange sight.

Josh turned around sharply at the noise of car tires screeching into the church parking lot. It was Frank Everett, just back from dropping off his mother-in-law at the Phoenix airport. Frank got down from his car, didn't bother even shutting the drivers' door and ran over to join them both by the admin building.

"What the . . . ?" he asked when he'd reached Josh and Connie, pointing over at the parsonage, which was mostly rubble now with an adamant wall or two standing amidst the ruins. "Did the kidnappers bomb the pastor's house to make their point?"

Connie shook her head and then laughed coldly. "It's a lot worse than that, man. Turns out that Pastor Fisher was your Judas Iscariot."

Frank just gaped at her, and then looked at her husband. "What?"

Josh nodded. "Yeah, dude, we've got a story to tell that you won't believe." He reached into his pocket and got out his cellphone. "But you're gonna have to wait till Detective Jenkins arrives to hear it."

CHAPTER 15

"I just can't believe it!" Detective Jenkins said as he and the others stood around the hidden parsonage basement, themselves in turn being surrounded by rubble and destroyed furniture. "Pastor Fisher and his wife were secretly worshipping the Devil?"

"I don't want to believe it either," Frank Everett said, placing a cautious foot on the cracked steel webbing that surrounded the hole and then gesturing down into it. "But the evidence is all down there."

Though the basement ceiling had fallen in and now obscured much of the floor, the Lord God had again clearly shown himself mighty, by defeating the traitorous pastor's plan to magically remove the evidence. The red pentagram-covered wallpaper was clearly evident, and one wall of the basement still had all of its shelves intact, complete with their gory satanic paraphernalia. Most damning of all was the metal statue of the Devil that stood in a corner, its twin in the opposite corner hidden under the fallen concrete.

"They also admitted to being the ones who were shutting down all the churches in town," Connie said.

"We tried to find out their plans," Josh added. "Why they were so insistent on closing down the church. But that's when he uttered that spell and the ceiling began collapsing in on us. And when our God sent his angel to—" Then he glanced at the detective's grim face and shrugged. "But you don't really believe that part of the story, do you, detective?"

"At the moment I've no idea what I believe anymore," Detective Jenkins said seriously, stroking his chin with his right thumb and forefinger. "Do I believe in God? Well, sure, it's the sane thing to do— I do think this universe we live in has an ultimate Creator. Do I believe in Jesus? 'Bout him coming to Earth to die for everyone's sins? Yeah, I guess I'm fine with that too." Then he gestured down into the parsonage basement. "But if you ask me if I believe in all *this* stuff . . . I mean, Pastor Fisher suddenly appearing like he's Obi Wan Kenobi and talking to you two and then uttering a spell that makes the whole building collapse . . . I'm gonna say, hey, gimme a break!" Then he laughed. "But, yeah, I'm also fine with God's angel appearing to save you guys, even though he won't be appearing in my official report either."

Everyone laughed uproariously at that. And while they laughed Josh thanked God for bringing them safely through this darkness and into His light and for revealing Satan's plans against the Joy of Life Bible Church.

Josh could see victory ahead for the church. The Black Circle organization would be back for certain— they didn't seem to ever quit—but God had already shown Himself to be much greater than them, and Josh was certain that the spiritual victory that he and Connie had in Christ would prove to be more than a match for all the forces of Hell combined.

The End

ABOUT THE AUTHOR

Gary Lee Vincent was born in Clarksburg, West Virginia and is an accomplished author, musician, actor, producer, director and entrepreneur. In 2010, his horror novel *Darkened Hills* was selected as 2010 Book of the Year winner by *Foreword Reviews Magazine* and became the pilot novel for *DARKENED - THE WEST VIRGINIA VAMPIRE SERIES*, that encompasses the novels *Darkened Hills, Darkened Hollows, Darkened Waters, Darkened Souls, Darkened Minds* and *Darkened Destinies*. He has also authored the bizarro thriller *Passageway,* a tribute to H.P. Lovecraft.

Gary co-authored the novel *Belly Timber* with John Russo, Solon Tsangaras, Dustin Kay and Ken Wallace, and co-authored the novel *Attack of the Melonheads* with Bob Gray and Solon Tsangaras.

As an actor, Gary has appeared in over seventy feature films and multiple television series, including *House of Cards*, *Mindhunter*, *The Walking Dead*, and *Stranger Things*.

As a director, Gary got his directorial debut with *A Promise to Astrid.* He has also directed the films *Desk Clerk*, *Dispatched*, *Midnight, Godsend,* and *Strange Friends.*

Also in Burning Bulb Publishing Christian Fantasy:

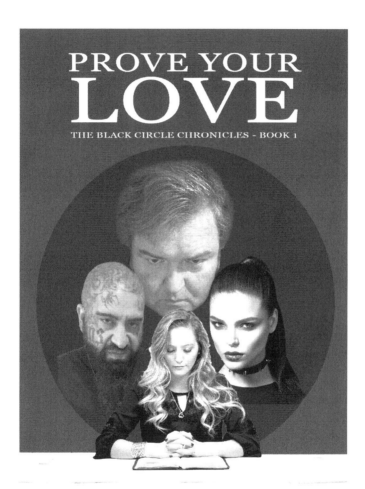

PROVE YOUR
LOVE

THE BLACK CIRCLE CHRONICLES - BOOK 1

GARY LEE VINCENT

GODSEND

RICH BOTTLES JR.

Made in the USA
Columbia, SC
27 September 2022